Blueberry Girl

Blueberry Girl

written by Neil Gaiman

illustrated by Charles Vess

BLOOMSBURY

LONDON BERLIN NEW YORK

Ladies
of
light
and
ladies
of
darkness
and
ladies
of
never-
you-
mind,

this is a prayer for a blueberry girl.

First, may
you
ladies
be kind.

Keep her from spindles and sleeps at sixteen,

let her stay waking and wise.

Nightmares at three or bad husbands at thirty,

These will not trouble her eyes.

Dull days at forty,
false friends at fifteen –
let her have
brave days
and
truth,

Let her go places
that we've never been,
trust and
delight
in
her
youth.

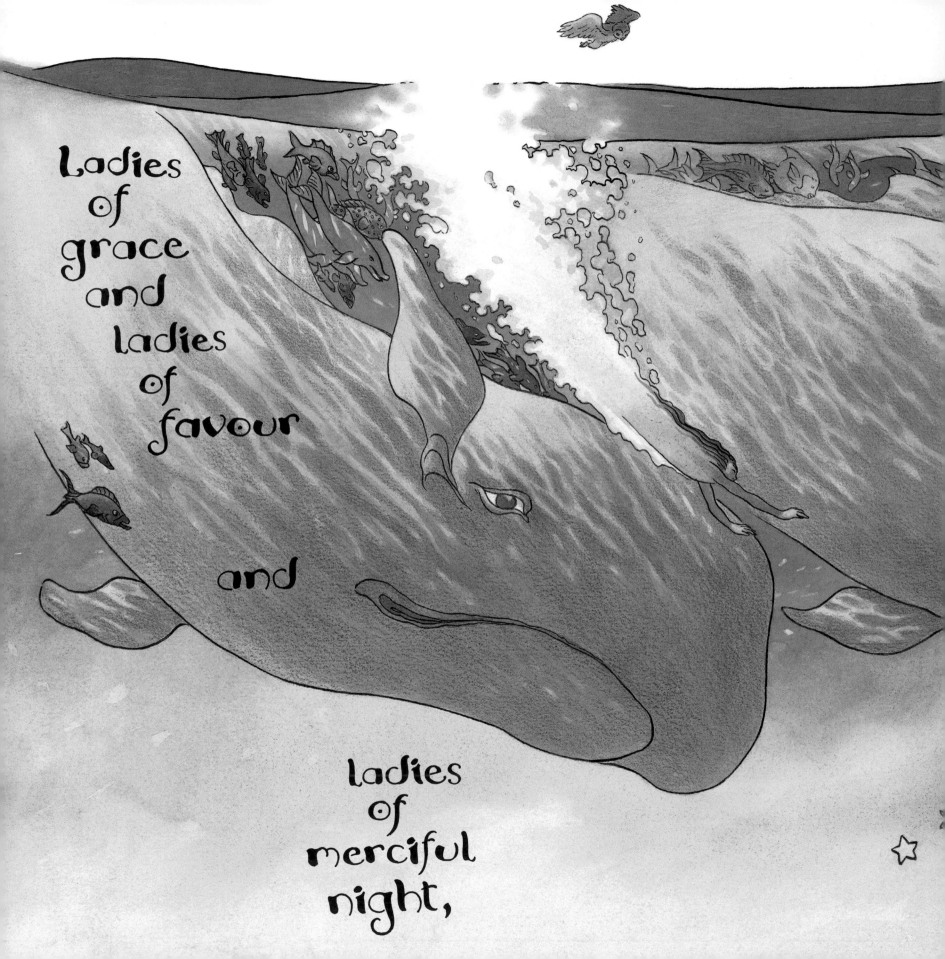

Ladies
of
grace
and
ladies
of
favour

and

ladies
of
merciful
night,

this is a prayer
for a blueberry girl.

Grant
her your
clearness
of
sight.

Words
can
be
worrisome,
people
complex,

motives
and
manners
unclear,

Grant her the wisdom to choose
her path right,

free from
unkindness
and fear.

Let her tell stories
and dance in the rain,
somersault,
tumble
and run,

her joys must be high as her sorrows are deep.

Let her grow like a weed in the sun.

Ladies
of
paradox,
ladies
of
measure,
ladies
of
shadows
that
fall,

this is a prayer
for a blueberry girl.

Words written clear on a wall.

Help her to help herself, help her to stand,

help her to lose and to find.

Teach her we're only as big as our dreams.

Show her that fortune is blind.

Truth is a thing she must find
for herself,
precious
and
rare
as
a
pearl.

Give
her
all
these
and a
little
bit
more...

Gifts for a blueberry girl.

I wrote this for Tori, and for Tash, when she was only a bump and a due date. With love, Neil

This one is for MY MOM, who was always there for me, MY first admirer and critic. All MY love from your son, Charles

Bloomsbury Publishing, London, Berlin and New York

First published in Great Britain in 2009 by Bloomsbury Publishing Plc
36 Soho Square, London, W1D 3QY

First published in the U.S. in 2009 by HarperCollins Children's Books
a division of HarperCollins Publishers, 1350 Avenue of the Americas, New York, NY 10019

Published by arrangement with HarperCollins Children's Books,
a division of HarperCollins Publishers

A CIP catalogue record of this book is available from the British Library

ISBN 978 0 7475 8616 6

Typography by Charles Vess

Printed in China by C&C offset

3 5 7 9 10 8 6 4 2

All papers used by Bloomsbury Publishing are natural, recyclable products
made from wood grown in well-managed forests. The manufacturing processes
conform to the environmental regulations of the country of origin

www.bloomsbury.com/childrens